Goober

Saddle Up Series
Book 29

Dave and Pat Sargent are longtime residents of Prairie Grove, Arkansas. Dave, a fourth-generation dairy farmer, began writing in early December 1990. Pat, a former teacher, began writing in the fourth grade. They enjoy the outdoors and have a real love for animals.

Goober

Saddle Up Series
Book 29

By Dave and Pat Sargent

Beyond "The End"
By Sue Rogers

Illustrated by Jane Lenoir

Ozark Publishing, Inc.
P.O. Box 228
Prairie Grove, AR 72753

Cataloging-in-Publication Data

Sargent, Dave, 1941—
    Goober / by Dave and Pat Sargent ;
illustrated by Jane Lenoir.—Prairie Grove, AR :
Ozark Publishing, c2004.
        p. cm. (Saddle up series ; 29)

    "Appreciate others"—Cover.
    SUMMARY: A silver dappled horse proudly
stands by his boss, George Washington Carver,
through good times and bad as he works to solve
the problems of Alabama farmers. Includes factual
information about silver dappled horses.
    ISBN 1-56763-689-6 (hc)
            1-56763-690-X (pbk)

    1. Horses—Juvenile fiction. [1. Horses—
Fiction. 2. Agriculture—Fiction. 3. Carver,
George Washington, 1864?-1943—Fiction.
4. Alabama—History—Fiction.] I. Sargent,
Pat, 1936– II. Lenoir, Jane, 1950– ill. III. Title.
IV. Series.

    PZ7.S2465Go 2004
    [Fic]—dc21   2001007598

Printed in the United States of America

Inspired by

cute little silver dappled Shetland ponies we see from time to time.

Dedicated to

our granddaughter,
Ashley Carrales,
who loves Shetland ponies.

Foreword

George Washington Carver, the educator, chemurgist, and botanist, is boss of Goober the silver dapple.

When Boss George teams up with Henry Ford, the silver dapple learns how smart his boss really is. They make rubber from the milk of the goldenrod plant. Imagine that!

Contents

If you would like to have the authors of the Saddle Up Series visit your school, free of charge, call 1-800-321-5671 or 1-800-960-3876.

One

George Washington Carver

Clouds drifted slowly across the Alabama countryside. As the sky darkened, a drizzle began falling. "Hmmm," Goober the silver dapple thought. "I know Boss is a mighty busy man, but I hope he isn't in that meeting in the Tuskegee Institute too much longer." He glanced at the large building in front of him, then turned his attention to the horse who was standing beside him and asked, "Do you suppose our bosses will be in there much longer?"

"They may," the dappled black grumbled. "My boss was really excited about the work your boss is doing with agriculture."

Goober swallowed to calm a sudden surge of pride before smiling and quietly muttering, "Thanks. He is a pretty smart fellow when it comes to plants and stuff."

"Humph," the dapple black snorted. "Smart? My boss says your boss is a genius, and that he's going to solve lots of problems for Alabama farmers."

A tear of pride joined the droplets of rain on the face of the proud silver dapple.

"I know he will do his best," Goober said. "He always has and always will. I really respect him. And I'll always give him my best."

Suddenly thunder rumbled in the distance, and streaks of lightning crisscrossed the southern sky.

"I hope," Goober whispered, "that he remembers his trusty horse standing in the rain waiting for him."

Suddenly the front door of the Institute opened, and several men hurried toward the long hitching rail. George Washington Carver quickly untied Goober's reins from the rail.

"Did you think I had forgotten you, my silver-dappled friend?" George said with a chuckle as he swung his right leg over the back of the saddle.

"Well now, Boss, to be honest, that thought did cross my mind," Goober muttered.

"Sorry," Boss George said as he reined Goober toward home. "But it's over now. Let's get you in a nice warm stall with fresh hay and a good helping of oats."

"Great! Now you're talking my language, Boss!" Goober nickered as he hit a fast trot toward home.

The rhythmic patter of rain-drops on the roof echoed through the cozy barn as George unsaddled his horse. He whistled cheerfully as he wiped the raindrops from the horse's wet coat with a dry cloth. His meeting had been a good one.

A moment later, George sat down on a bale of hay and leaned back against the wall.

After a sigh, he said, "Goober, I came from very humble beginnings. My papa and mama were slaves. I was kidnapped by some bad men, and Moses Carver paid those kid-nappers a three-hundred-dollar horse to get me back."

"Wow, Boss!" Goober snorted. "That's a lot of money!"

George stroked Goober's nose for a moment before adding, "I went to a one-room school, and I was later turned away from a fine university because of my race." He chuckled and stood up. "But now, that act didn't stop me from graduating from Simpson and Ames later. And now," he said as he paced back and forth in the horse stall, "I have been asked by Mr. Booker T. Washington to head the agriculture department at the Tuskegee Institute."

"Great!" Goober neighed. "I hope you take the position."

"Of course, I will gladly accept the invitation," George said. "It will give me the opportunity to discover new and better ways of farming."

The man yawned. "But right now, we'd better get some sleep. Good night, Goober. Hope you have pleasant dreams. I know I will."

Goober smiled and nodded his head as he watched his boss disappear into the stormy night.

"I am one lucky horse," Goober murmured as he drifted off into a peaceful sleep. "My boss is a good man, a brilliant botanist, and an exciting and wonderful partner."

It was three hours later when a bolt of lightning crashed through the night, shattering Goober's pleasant dreams.

The silver dapple jumped to his feet. First, his ears shot forward, then flattened back against his head as the barn shook with a powerful explosion of thunder.

A very frightened horse raced to the door to check for damages. Wide eyed and snorting with fear, he looked toward the house where George was sleeping. Flames were leaping high into the sky, and smoke billowed from the burning home.

"Fire!" he neighed. "Boss!"
His heart pounded with fear as he raced into the storm-riddled night.

Two

The Rescue

Seconds later, the silver dapple was rearing on his hind legs as his front hooves lashed against the front door of the house. The pungent odor of burning wood poured through the doorway as the door splintered into a million pieces. Smoke burned his eyes as he stumbled into the flaming structure.

"Boss!" he neighed loudly. "Where are you?" He coughed and then tried to hold his breath as he stumbled from room to room.

"Boss, say something so I can find you," he pleaded as he bumped against tables and chairs, frantically trying to locate him.

Suddenly a flash of lightning illuminated the interior of the house, and he saw George through the heavy blanket of smoke. He was leaned against a wall, and his eyes were closed. Goober noticed a trail of red on his white nightshirt.

"Oh no," he gasped. "Boss is hurt. He will never make it out of here alive unless...unless..."

Goober began to feel dizzy. "I must hurry," he thought. "The smoke is too thick for me to breathe. I'm going to pass out if I don't get some fresh air inside my lungs." Staggering back onto the front porch, he breathed deeply several times. Then, whirling around and racing back into the burning house, he ran straight toward his friend.

Grabbing his shirt collar with his teeth, the silver dapple slowly backed out of the room with the unconscious body of George trailing along behind.

Goober's ears were flat against the back of his head as he stumbled backward through the flames and falling embers. "Just a little farther, Goober," he silently told himself. "Just a little farther. You can do it. The life of your boss depends on you reaching that front porch and fresh air." He tried to avoid looking at the big cut on George's head. He tried to ignore the smell of his scorched hair and the pain within his lungs. "Step back," he silently commanded. "One more step. Just one more step." It seemed like a dream as Goober carefully inched his way along. Suddenly he realized that he was stepping down. He looked down to see where he was, and he saw that George was sliding down the steps of the front porch.

"W-w-we made it, B-boss!" he groaned. "We made it!"

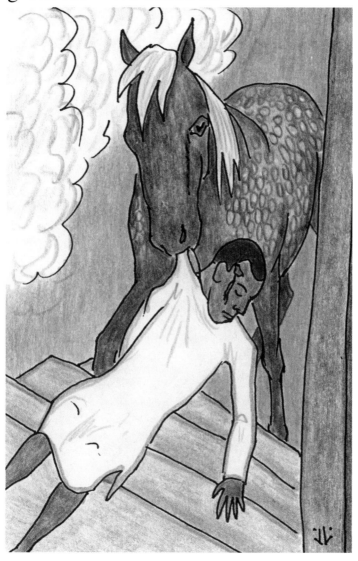

He gently released his gripping teeth from George's collar, and the man collapsed upon the soggy grass. Goober gently nuzzled his ear and cheek, but George did not respond.

"You just have to be alive, George Washington Carver Boss. You have many great things to do yet. I'll go for a doctor," Goober said frantically. "Don't move. I'll be right back, Boss." He nuzzled the unconscious man on his cheek before adding, "That was silly of me, wasn't it, Boss? Of course you won't move. Just keep breathing."

Four hours later, the storm had passed, and the moon was shining brightly upon the wet Alabama countryside.

The silver dapple was standing outside the neighbor's bedroom where George had been taken by the doctor.

"I appreciate your good work, Doc," George said. "I'm feeling a lot better now."

"Don't appreciate my work, George," the doctor said with a big chuckle. "Just thank your lucky stars that Goober saved you from that burning house."

With a big smile, George said, "Thanks, Goober. I'll do something special for you when I get better."

"You don't need to do anything special, Boss," the silver dapple muttered. "Just get well and go to work with Booker T. Washington. That will be payment enough for me."

Three

Goldenrod Milk to Rubber

Goober and his boss spent the following three years experimenting with the Alabama soil. George added minerals by planting nitrogen-producing legumes. And he also discovered that sweet potatoes and peanuts were very high-yielding crops for the area.

One morning Goober saw his boss walking toward the corral with a frown on his face. "This is unusual," the silver dapple thought. "He's always smiling and happy."

"Hi, Boss," he nickered loudly. "Beautiful day, isn't it?"

George silently saddled him before speaking his thoughts.

"Goober, farmers agree that peanuts and sweet potatoes grow good in this Alabama soil."

"They should, Boss," Goober muttered with a nod of his head. "You have already proven that."

"But," George added as he slipped his boot in the stirrup and mounted, "they can't find a good market for either one. I have to help them with this problem. There has to be more to sweet potatoes and peanuts than meets the eye."

"You'll find other uses for them," the silver dapple nickered. "I know you will, Boss."

For several weeks, Goober watched his boss experiment with a sweet potato and a peanut. Then he heard the words that he was waiting for.

"Goober, there are more than three hundred uses for peanuts and sweet potatoes besides the obvious!"

"Awesome!" the silver dapple neighed. "So what are we going to do now, Boss? Are we going to take a vacation?"

The silver dapple and his boss were on their way home when they met a smutty olive grullo and his boss, Henry Ford, on the road.

"I have been looking for you, George," Henry said with a smile. "I need your help."

Goober looked at the smutty olive grullo and said, "Your boss is in a different business than mine. How can my boss help him?"

"That's what I was wondering," the grullo muttered. "My boss builds engines, and yours grows plants. I don't see any connection."

"Hmmm," Goober murmured. "This may be interesting."

Several weeks later, Goober and the smutty olive grullo were waiting at the hitching rail in front of the Tuskegee Institute.

Suddenly the door flew open. George Washington Carver and Henry Ford walked toward their horses with smiles on their faces.

"George Washington Carver," Henry said, "you are an amazing man. Who would have thought that rubber could be made from the milk of the goldenrod!"

George shook hands and said, "Never underestimate the miracles offered by our plant life, Henry. I've enjoyed working with you."

"It looks like our bosses work together real good," the grullo said.

"It sure does," Goober agreed. He nuzzled the horse on the neck. "I enjoyed visiting with you, Grullo."

A moment before Henry Ford and the smutty olive grullo left, Goober nickered, "My boss will meet your boss in the history books. I don't think either one of them will ever be forgotten, do you?"

"Nope," the grullo answered. "They are both changing the world."

"That may be right," Goober mumbled. "You think your boss is the greatest, and I think my boss is the greatest! We're both correct!"

He thought that he heard the smutty olive grullo mutter something as he trotted away, but he wasn't sure.

George Washington Carver stroked Goober's neck and said, "I'm a lucky man. Understanding plants and nature is natural for me, Goober. Meeting and working with great people is a wonderful bonus."

"Hmmm," Goober thought. "George Washington Carver will go down in history as a great botanist, chemurgist, and educator. But I wonder if folks will remember his silver dapple named Goober."

"Well, I guess that's not what is important. My life is good. It's a new adventure every day!"

Four

Silver Dapple Facts

Silver dapple is a special color. It is sometimes confused with chestnut. There are several varieties of breeds in Europe that are considered silver dapple, but in the United States silver dapple occurs only in Shetland ponies.

Dappling is the pattern created when darker areas overlie lighter areas. Any color of horse can be dappled, even black. Dappling is caused by differences in hair color on some parts of the skin.

Dappling shows more when horses shed their hair coats in spring and fall, but it is always present on greys and silver dapples.

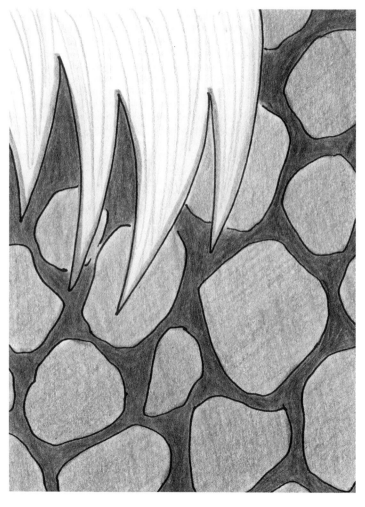

BEYOND "THE END"

Do not underestimate a horse's pride,
or he will dent yours.

Anonymous

WORD LIST
silver dapple
dandy brush
anvil
Shetland
shoe puller
dappled black
Chincoteague
rasp
rubber currycomb
Hackney
smutty olive grullo
horseshoe
sweatscraper
chestnut

hammer
Welsh Mountain
nails
body brush
seal brown pony
hoof buffer
sponge

From the word list above, write:

1. Four names for breeds of ponies.

2. Five names for color types of ponies.

3. Seven pieces of equipment a black-smith or farrier uses.

4. Five pieces of equipment used to groom a pony.

Tell the purpose and use of each piece of grooming equipment.

CURRICULUM CONNECTIONS

How high does a pony measure?

What does "mucking out" a stall mean?

Was George Washington Carver a real person? Is there a real college named Tuskegee Institute in Alabama? Yes! George Washington Carver was a real person, and he did discover more than 300 uses for peanuts and sweet potatoes (Try Sweet Potato Pie—recipe at <www. recipesource.com/text./baked-goods/ desserts/pies/ recipe529. txt>.) Yes, there is a real college named Tuskegee Institute. It was founded in 1881 by Booker T. Washington and is still an active institution today. Buildings built with bricks made by students in the Institute's brickyard are preserved and used today.

Then did this story actually happen? Is it fact, or is it a fiction story based on actual people and a period of time? What type of story is it?

Make up a story about one day when the kilns would not heat to make bricks the students needed to build the home of Booker T. Washington. What type of story will this be?

PROJECT

Combine your math and artistic skills! Draw to scale and accurately color a picture (body, tail, and mane) of the horse that is featured in each book read in the Saddle Up Series. You could soon have sixty horses prancing around the walls of your classroom!

Learning + horses = FUN.

Look in your school library media center for books about how to draw a horse and the colors of horses. Don't forget the useful information in the last chapter of this book (Silver Dapple Facts) and the picture on the book cover for a shape and color guide.

HELPFUL HINTS AND WEBSITES

A horse is measured in hands. One hand equals four inches. Use a scale of 1" equals 1 hand.

Visit website <www.equisearch.com> to find a glossary of equine terms, information about tack and equipment, breeds, art and graphics, and more about horses. Learn more at <www.horse-country. com> and at <www.ansi.okstate.edu/ breeds/horses/>. KidsClick! is a web search for kids by librarians. There are many interesting websites here. HORSES and HORSEMANSHIP are two of the more than 600 subjects. Visit <www. kidsclick.org>. Is your classroom beginning to look like the Rocking S Horse Ranch? Happy Trails to You!

ANSWERS (1. Ponies measure 14 hands and 2 inches, or less. 2. Mucking out means lifting out the manure and wet bedding with a pitchfork. 3. It is a fiction story based on fact, called Historical Fiction. Your story about the bricks will be Historical Fiction, also—a fiction story based on fact.)